The Girl Who Loved Caterpillars

ADAPTED BY **JEAN MERRILL** • ILLUSTRATED BY **FLOYD COOPER**

A TWELFTH-CENTURY TALE FROM JAPAN

PHILOMEL BOOKS • NEW YORK

Text copyright © 1992 by Jean Merrill

Illustrations copyright © 1992 by Floyd Cooper

Philomel Books, a division of The Putnam & Grosset Group,

200 Madison Avenue, New York, NY 10016

All rights reserved. This book, or parts thereof, may not be

reproduced in any form without permission from the publisher.

Published simultaneously in Canada.

Printed in Hong Kong by South China Printing Co. (1988), Ltd.

Book design by Nanette Stevenson. Lettering by David Gatti.

The text is set in Cloister.

Library of Congress Cataloging-in-Publication Data

Merrill, Jean. The girl who loved caterpillars :

a twelfth-century tale from Japan / adapted by Jean Merrill ;

illustrated by Floyd Cooper. p. cm.

Adaptation of an anonymous story in the *Tsutsumi Chūnagon Monogatari*.

Summary: In this retelling of an anonymous twelfth-century

Japanese story, the young woman Izumi resists social and family pressures

as she befriends caterpillars and other socially unacceptable creatures.

[1. Japan—Fiction. 2. Conduct of life—Fiction.]

I. Cooper, Floyd, ill. II. *Tsutsumi Chūnagon Monogatari*. III. Title.

PZ7.M5357Gi 1992 [E]—dc20 91-29054 CIP AC ISBN 0-399-21871-8

The Girl Who Loved Caterpillars, an adaptation of an anonymous twelfth-century Japanese story in the *Tsutsumi Chūnagon Monogatari*, is based on the following three English translations: "The Lady Who Loved Worms," by Edwin O. Reischauer and Joseph K. Yamagiwa, in *Translations from Early Japanese Literature* (Harvard University Press, 1951); "The Lady Who Loved Insects," by Arthur Waley, in *The Real Tripitaka and Other Pieces* (George Allen & Unwin, 1952); and "The Young Lady Who Loved Insects," by Umeyo Hirano, in *Tsutsumi Chūnagon Monogatari* (The Hokuseido Press, 1963). The artist used an oil wash on board to prepare the illustrations for this book. The artwork was then scanned by laser and separated into four colors for reproduction on sheet-fed offset printing presses.

3 5 7 9 10 8 6 4 2

A "for you" for Marge—J.M.

For Mamiko, Robyn, John, Nanette, Patti, and Junko,
for making the journey possible.—F.C.

Izumi was her name. But she was known as The Girl Who Loved Caterpillars.

Izumi was the only daughter of a provincial inspector, who served in the Emperor's court in Kyoto some eight hundred years ago. The court was one of great elegance, and the Inspector had friends in the highest circles and hoped in time to be made Inspector General of all the provinces.

Izumi was a pretty girl—and clever. And it was her parents' hope that she might become a lady-in-waiting in the Emperor's court, or that she might marry a nobleman of high rank.

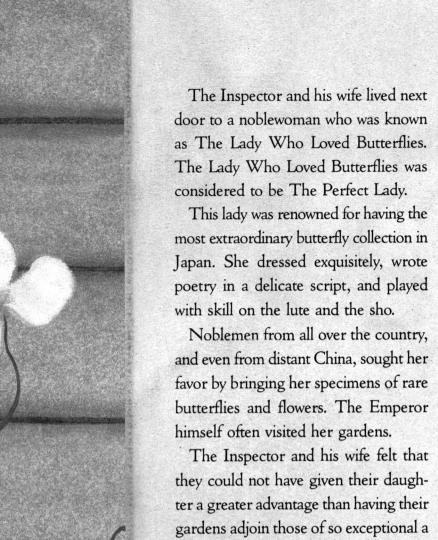

The Inspector and his wife lived next door to a noblewoman who was known as The Lady Who Loved Butterflies. The Lady Who Loved Butterflies was considered to be The Perfect Lady.

This lady was renowned for having the most extraordinary butterfly collection in Japan. She dressed exquisitely, wrote poetry in a delicate script, and played with skill on the lute and the sho.

Noblemen from all over the country, and even from distant China, sought her favor by bringing her specimens of rare butterflies and flowers. The Emperor himself often visited her gardens.

The Inspector and his wife felt that they could not have given their daughter a greater advantage than having their gardens adjoin those of so exceptional a model of womanly charm.

But when Izumi's friends carried on about the famous lady next door, Izumi would look at them wonderingly.

"Why," she asked, "do people make such a fuss about butterflies and pay no attention to the creatures from which butterflies come? It is caterpillars that are really interesting."

From the time she could walk, Izumi had delighted in worms, toads, insects, and all sorts of creatures that most people disliked to touch. Her room was filled with boxes and baskets of crawling, squirming, hopping creatures. She spent hours observing their movements and watching how they grew.

The caterpillars were her favorites. Izumi would lie on the floor of her room, studying a furry worm as it inched its way up her arm.

Most of the girls Izumi knew were squeamish about caterpillars and puzzled by her fascination with them. Izumi's preferred companions were some scruffy-looking boys from families of low standing. Izumi had no lack of admirers among these boys. They came to her window at all hours, bringing caterpillars and other insects that they knew would interest her.

If the boys did not know the names of the creatures they brought her, Izumi would invent names for them. A rhinoceros beetle she called One Horn. A tree frog was called Spring Song.

Izumi also made up names for the boys. Her favorites among her friends, she called Worm Boy, Mantis Man, and Centipede.

The Inspector and his wife were embarrassed to have these ragged, dirty boys always hanging about their gardens. And to hear Izumi addressing them by such vulgar names added to their distress.

"How can the name of a natural thing be vulgar?" Izumi inquired. "We may all be centipedes in our next life. Perhaps we were all toads in our previous life."

Izumi hated anything that was not natural. She refused to pluck her eyebrows into a fine thin line as other girls did. She let her brows grow full and hairy as a caterpillar's back.

And her teeth were a pure, naked, natural white, although it was the fashion at the time for ladies to blacken their teeth. Izumi refused to paint her teeth. She said that this was an unnatural custom.

"Why can you not be like other girls?" the Inspector and his wife pleaded with Izumi. "We, of course, love you as you are, bushy eyebrows and all. But people like things of a pleasing appearance. And when they hear about your keeping hairy caterpillars, your chances of attracting young men of noble families will be damaged."

"I don't care about that," Izumi said. "Flowers and butterflies are pretty, but not nearly as interesting as seeds or caterpillars. It's the original nature of things that I wish to know about."

Izumi explained her ideas so reasonably that her parents had the uneasy feeling that she might be cleverer than they. But they were aware that their neighbors considered Izumi an odd girl.

The ladies-in-waiting who served in the Inspector's household joined in the gossip about Izumi. They felt that it did not add to their standing to be working for the family of The Girl Who Loved Caterpillars.

Several of them wrote verses complaining of their misfortune.

One lady-in-waiting wrote:

How did I come
of my own free will
to work in a house where
I must wait on caterpillars?

Another lamented:

How lucky they are next door.
They talk of flowers and butterflies,
while we work in rooms
that stink of caterpillars.

A lady-in-waiting who served in the house of The Lady Who Loved Butterflies tried to cheer up her friends next door with the thought:

When winter comes,
no matter how cold,
you will be well off for clothes.
With all those caterpillars,
you can make yourselves fur coats.

Such comments only made Izumi defend the charms of her caterpillars more stubbornly.

As the daughter of an important official, Izumi was given many beautiful presents by persons who wished to win favor with her father. But Izumi did not care much for possessions, and she often gave away her expensive gifts to the boys who collected insects for her.

One day a report of Izumi's strange ways reached a young nobleman who had never met a young lady who was not frightened by creeping, crawling things. He could not believe Izumi was as fearless as she sounded.

The young man made a large and marvelously lifelike snake with joints that moved. He put the snake in a sack with a scale-like pattern and had it delivered to Izumi with a message that read:

Creeping and crawling,
I have snaked my way to your side,
and I will be as faithful
as my body is long.

The ladies-in-waiting who delivered the sack to Izumi had no idea what it contained. When they untied the sack and the head of the mechanical snake poked out, the ladies screamed.

Izumi was startled, but smiled and recited a prayer to Buddha.

"We must not be afraid," she told the trembling ladies-in-waiting. "Any one of us may have been a snake in a former life. For my part, I consider him a relative."

Izumi turned to one of her caterpillars. "And you, small furry worm, do you think this fellow is one of your relatives?"

But for all her brave words, Izumi was uneasy. The snake was a thousand times larger than her caterpillars. As she pulled the sack closer, she sang to the snake in a low voice to calm it.

Izumi's singing to the snake struck the ladies-in-waiting as both frightening and hilarious, and they rushed out of the room giggling and squealing.

They collided in the hall with the Inspector who was shocked to hear that the serving women had run off leaving his daughter closeted with a huge snake.

The Inspector seized his sword and rushed to Izumi's room. He was about to cut off the snake's head, when he realized that it was not a real snake, but a cleverly made toy. Much relieved, he laughed heartily at the joke that had been played.

On learning the name of the nobleman who had made the snake, the Inspector told Izumi, "I have often heard how clever this fellow is at making such things. No doubt he has heard of your serious studies of strange creatures and thought to delight you with his good imitation. You must, of course, write and thank him for his kindness."

Izumi, although a little disappointed that the snake was not a real one, agreed with her father that so ingenious a present deserved a reply.

Any other young lady writing to a nobleman would have written in beautiful script on the finest rice paper. Izumi simply printed on cardboard in her bold, plain handwriting this message:

> *Dear Snake Man—*
> *Oh, clever imitator of snakes,*
> *you and I may not be fated*
> *to meet on this earth.*
> *But in another life,*
> *I may recognize you as a snake.*
> *What paradise!*

When this note was delivered, the young man who had made the snake showed it to a friend, a Captain of the Stables. The Captain was curious about the girl who had responded so wittily to his friend's joke and decided he must see her for himself.

He went to Izumi's house and hid in the garden outside her window. There he saw a gang of boys poking about in the bushes, and he heard one of them call out, "Come over here! This bush is covered with caterpillars."

The other boys raced over to look. Then one of them ran to Izumi's window.

"Izumi," he called. "Come look! There are hundreds of the most beautiful caterpillars you have ever seen."

The Captain held his breath as Izumi pulled aside the window blind and leaned out to look.

Izumi was carelessly dressed, as if she had not thought much about what clothes she had on, and her hair was flying every which way. She looked like some wild creature of the woods.

The Captain thought—if she were to pin up her hair, blacken her teeth, and pluck her eyebrows, she would be considered one of the most beautiful ladies in the Emperor's court. But in truth the Captain did not find her unattractive as she was.

He was struck by her dark, luxuriant eyebrows and flashing, white teeth. He noted the fresh color of her cheeks, the brightness of her eyes, and the sweetness of her smile. And the short jacket with a cricket design that she wore over a silk robe was very becoming.

The Captain listened to the excitement in the girl's voice as she exclaimed over the caterpillars.

"How clever they are," she said. "They have crawled into that bush to get out of the broiling sun. Do collect some and bring them here so I can examine them.

"Don't let them fall!" she called, as the boys pulled at a branch of the bush.

When several caterpillars did fall with a plop to the ground, Izumi passed one of the boys a white silk fan. "Place them gently on the fan and hand it up to me," she said.

But as Izumi was reaching down, one of the boys caught sight of the Captain hiding by the gate and called out a warning.

One of the ladies-in-waiting came rushing to Izumi's room to find her young mistress leaning out the window in full view of a strange young nobleman.

"Come away from the window at once," the serving woman begged.

"Don't be silly," Izumi said. "I'm not doing anything to be ashamed of." But she dropped the window blind to carry her caterpillars in out of the sun.

The Captain felt that he should apologize to Izumi for having stared at her. He took a folded paper from his pocket and, using the juice of a flower stem as ink, he wrote:

Caterpillar Girl—
Forgive me for standing
at your gate so long.
Having seen you with your brows
thick as a caterpillar's fur,
I shall carry that picture
with me always.

The Captain summoned one of the boys and asked him to deliver the note. The boy went to the window and called Izumi.

The lady-in-waiting raised the blind and snatched the paper from the boy's hand. When she looked at the message, she recognized the name of the Captain.

"Oh, unfortunate girl," she sighed. "A great nobleman has seen you messing with your revolting worms. Your father's house will be the joke of the court."

Izumi looked up from her caterpillars and said mildly, "If you looked at more than the surface of things, perhaps you would not mind what people thought of you."

One of the boys called from the garden that the Captain was waiting, hoping there might be an answer to his note.

"You must, at least, write a polite reply," the lady-in-waiting told Izumi.

Izumi smiled and wrote:

> As you see,
> I am not like other girls.
> And had you not called me
>   Caterpillar,
> I would not have replied.
> What should I call you?

The Captain, on reading Izumi's reply, sent back another note:

What use to tell you my name?
Alas, I fear no man exists
sensitive and brave enough
to tune his life to a caterpillar.
Farewell, Caterpillar Girl.

And the Captain went his way, amused and wondering.

For a moment, he fancied he heard Izumi calling after him. But she was calling to one of the boys in the garden.

"Worm Boy," she was saying, "I need fresh leaves for the caterpillars."

Afterword

Izumi's story, believed to have been written in the twelfth century (Heian Period), may have been part of a much longer story about Japanese court life. The author, whose name is unknown, ended the account with the teasing promise: "What happened next will be found in the second chapter."

But if there was another chapter, it has been lost. Did Izumi become a scientist? A philosopher? Did the Captain ever return? Or did Izumi further scandalize her family by running off with Worm Boy or Mantis Man?

Whatever her fate, twentieth-century champions of women's liberation could not wish for a better example than the free-spirited "girl who loved caterpillars," who went her own way in a time when young women's roles were much more circumscribed than they are today.